Carol-Ann Jensen

*To Norma,
Friends Forever from
Gooding - Class of '55*

Night of the Thunder Moon

Carol-Ann

Illustrated by Lance Quinn

Night of the Thunder Moon

Moonstone Publishing
Copyright © 2017
All Rights Reserved

C.A.J. & L. Q.

Acknowledgements

With love and our deepest thanks to our families for their endless patience and understanding throughout the creation of this fun book.

Also, special thanks to the editorial team, without whom this book would still be only a dream and a wish:

- Dr. Ron Brown
- Dr. Gavin Harper
- Mattie Ann Fuller
- Aurora Quinn
- Jensen Quinn
- Brea Quinn
- Denise Stark
- Robert J. Fuller

We appreciate your support, encouragement, and sacrifices.

C.A.J. & L. Q.

"Don't ever call me Levina again!" screamed the feisty, seven-year-old girl. Nine-year-old Jake delighted in teasing his little sister.

"Just because I have a dumb name like Levina, you don't have to rub it in! Call me Levi, or I'll never let you look at my dinosaur book again."

"I don't even care a whit about your book. Look at these nifty dinosaurs I found in the cereal box this morning." Jake knew he held a treasure in his hand because everybody in school had dinosaur toys in the 1950s. "Nanny-Nanny Billy Goat, my toys are better than your book."

"Will you two quit fighting?" insisted their mother. "I am tired of listening to your wrangling and jangling. One more word of quarreling and neither of you will go to the rodeo tonight to watch your dad."

Their dad, a saddle bronc rider, was vying for championship points on the circuit.

A good ride tonight would put him in the finals tomorrow night at the Toponis County Fair & Rodeo, one of Idaho's premium rodeos. Both kids were excited and eager to cheer for him, but they kept picking and poking at each other.

The two kids jostled out of their trailer parked behind the chutes, still bickering and squabbling. Other cowboys could hear their foofaraw and rumpus all over the campground as Levi and Jake stomped past Dad's new '55 Chevy pickup. They headed for the stadium to watch the Heavyweight-Horse Pulling contest and 4-H tractor pulls in the arena.

"I'll race you," taunted mischievous Jake, knowing full well he could beat his little sister. Running across the camping lot, Levi stepped in a hole and tumbled head over teakettle.

"JACOB--!" Levi screamed, using his full name for emphasis. She clumped down in a heap and cried; Jake kept running. Tear-streaked and dirty, Levi hobbled back to the trailer.

"That's it!" declared Mother. "Neither of you can go to the rodeo tonight. I'll ask Sadie from the next trailer to check on both of you." In the 1950s, many of the rodeo folks on the circuit parked their trucks and trailers out in back of the chutes and kept an eye out for each other.

At 7:00, Mom and Dad headed to the chutes. Walking out the door, Mom reminded them, "You two stay in this trailer and **NO** fighting. You hear? If you want to go tomorrow night to watch the championships, you better learn to get along tonight." Levi and Jake glared at each other across the table.

Finally, Levi picked up her book, flipped through the pages, and ignored her brother.

Jake pulled out his toy horses, cowboys, and two new dinosaurs, but he wasn't having fun. "If you treat me better, I'll share my *Tyrannosaurus* and *Brontosaurus* dinosaurs with you."

"I'll be nice to you if you'll be nice to me," she said. Levi studied every page and discovered that dinosaurs flaunted many colors such as browns, greens, blues, and reds. All of a sudden, Levi burst out with the giggles. "Jake, come look at this word I just found about dinosaurs: *coprolite*. It means fossilized dinosaur poop!"

Laughing together broke the tension, and peace slowly crept back into the trailer. They could hear the rodeo announcer's voice booming through the night air.

"Ladies and Gentlemen . . . Kids and Dogs . . . ," he chanted over the microphone. "Let's put our hands together to welcome tonight's cowboys and cowgirls." John Phillip Sousa's rousing music blared over the loudspeaker system; Jake and Levi could imagine the Grand Entry, the parade of all the rodeo people.

Leading the curvy, serpentine line of horses, cowboys, and the Toponis County Posse would be the Rodeo Queen carrying the American flag, wind-swaying out behind her.

Galloping in a long, flowing line would be pretty girls bearing banners and flags, followed by cowboys, cowgirls, pick-up men, and clowns.

Hoofbeats pounded around the arena, drumming up excitement for the performers. The excited crowd of local folks and visitors, all decked out in their best blue jeans, shirts, boots, and brims, filled the wooden benches.

They stood tall, cheered, and clapped for the Grand Entry. As their red, white, and blue American flag traveled around the arena, every single person put their hands on their hearts and sang the National Anthem with pride and gusto.

"Golly, I wish I could watch Daddy ride," whimpered Levi.

"Me too," grumbled Jake. "Let's listen to the announcer, and at least we can pretend we're watching."

They heard the crowd erupt with laughter. "I bet the clown wearing the red wig and polka dot pants with suspenders just told his silly joke," guessed Jake.

They both remembered last night's performance when the clown shouted at the announcer from the middle of the ring and said, "How did the dinosaur skeleton know it was going to rain?"

"I don't know," responded the announcer over the loud speaker. "You tell us. The crowd wants to know."

"He felt it in his bones," chortled the clown. Some of the crowd laughed; some groaned.

"Yeah, and I love it when the clown hops in the rubber barrel and bugs the mad Brahma bulls," added Jake. The kids knew the clowns were always funny, but they also knew that sometimes their antics were for the safety of the riders. Clowns often ran in front of a mad bull to detract it from the cowboy and protect him as he scrambled out of harm's way.   Sometimes the funny men even cleaned up the horse droppings so riders wouldn't fall in a stinky pile if they were bucked off their mounts.

Darkness settled. Floodlights lit the arena, bright as day, and the moon lit the heavens. As a warm summer breeze wafted through the window, both kids caught an aroma of grilled hamburgers with fried onions.

"Darn, those burgers smell yummy. I wish we were over there!" muttered Jake again.

"Let's look at my book together now, Jake," said Levi.

"Tomorrow night we will be there to watch Daddy win."

Levi and Jake flipped through the book. "Look at this *Brontosaurus*!" exclaimed Jake. "He looks just like the toy I found in the cereal box. This book says he weighed up to 17 tons, Levi."

"How big is that?"

Jake explained, "That many tons equal 20 full grown Brahma bulls or 25 bucking horses like Dad rides. Can you imagine that many big horses or Brahmas running loose through this campground at the same time? That would really rattle our trailer. No wonder the *Brontosaurus* is called a *Thunder Lizard*. When he clomped around looking for food, he shook the earth."

Jake handed his toy to Levi and let her clomp it on the table.

"Wow! What if this *Brontosaurus* came to life right now?" said Levi. "Daddy says some Indians call this full moon in the July sky the *Thunder Moon*. If the Thunder Moon brings this Thunder Lizard back to life, what will you do?"

"I'll tell you what I'll do," bragged the big brother as the two kids envisioned themselves competing at a giant dinosaur rodeo. "I'll throw my bareback rigging behind his big head and cinch it up tight. I'll hop right up on the skinny part of his neck, lock my spurs on him, and hang on for one hallacious bareback ride!"

"Oh, Jake," said the little sister, opening her big eyes wide. "Won't you be scared?"

"I bet when I ride that old Thunder Lizard into the arena at that Dinosaur Rodeo I will hear every one of those folks up in the stands cheering like crazy. Just look at me, Levi. Can you see me straddling the gigantic Bronto, my hat pulled down, one hand gripping my rigging, and the other hand reaching for the moon?"

Levi tried to imagine her brother straddling a colossal lizard. Jake went on describing his ride. "I'll be decked out in my spiffy white shirt, my new blue jeans, and leather chaps. Then I will holler to make sure you are watching me. From the top of that Thunder Lizard I will shove my arm in the air and hang on."

The image of the toy dinosaur danced in the light from the Thunder Moon on the trailer window. The children looked through the reflection towards the arena. Soon the tiny *Brontosaurus* transformed into a massive, life-sized, mottled-blue reptile. It gaped its massive mouth and roared. . .

"Our champion *Brontosaurus* bareback rider tonight, Ladies and Gentlemen," boomed the announcer, "is a young man who hails right out of Hailey, Idaho . . . *Jacob Lundlie*! Let him hear your voices. Bring this gritty rider into the arena with your cheers!!"

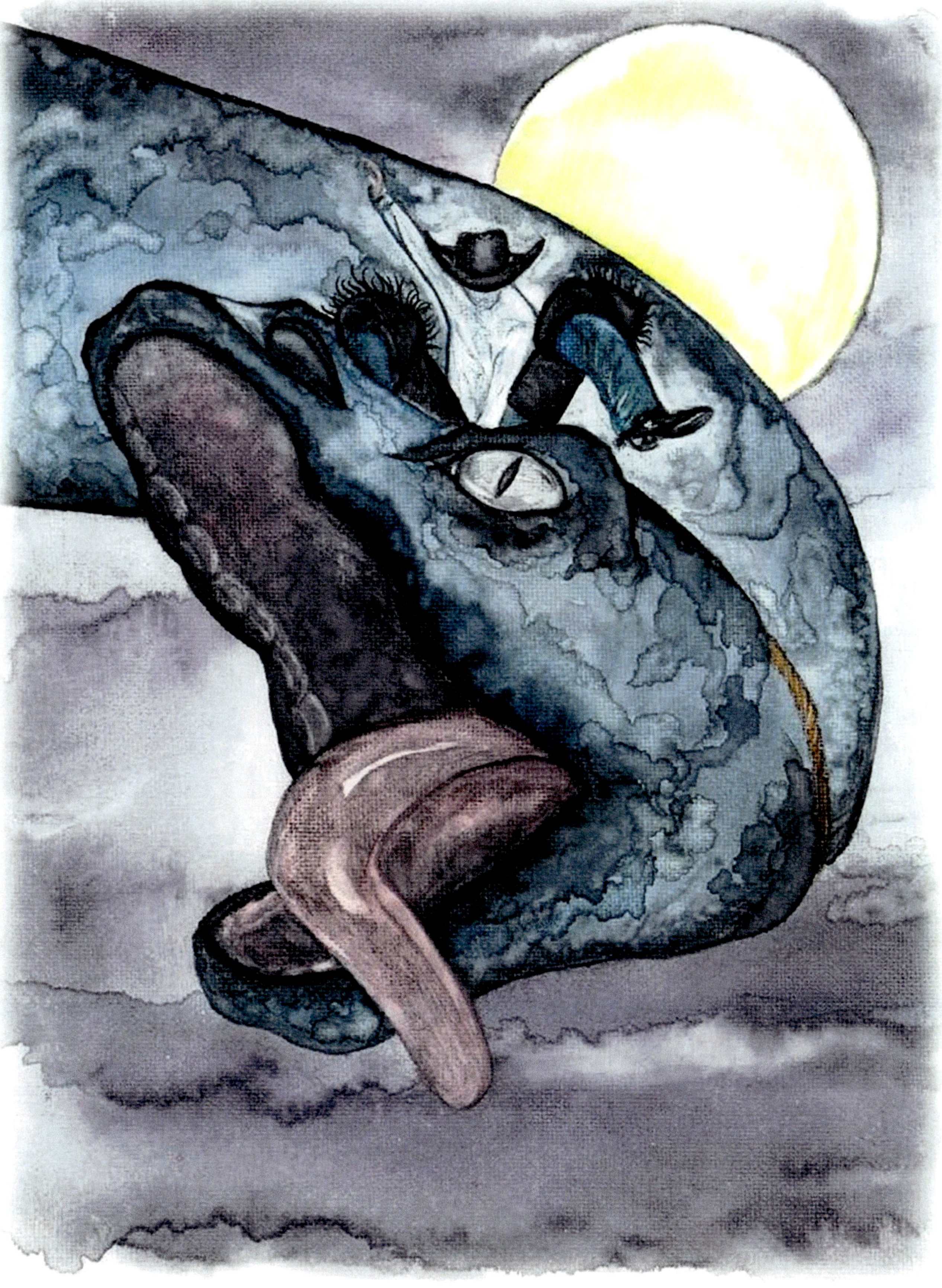

Levi heard the crowd roar as her brother rode the 70-foot hunk of angry dinosaur. Jake lost his hat but made the eight-second ride. The plucky rider heard the buzzer squawk and bailed off into the soft sand.

The pick-up men rode into the arena and headed the snorting Thunder Lizard down to the holding pens at the far end. Jake grabbed his hat out of the dirt, dusted himself off, waved at the crowd, and headed back to the chutes.

As the crowd settled in, the announcer introduced a specialty act. Brother and sister perched on the gates watching two trick riders lope into the arena, each on her own bulky *Stegosaurus*.

"Ladies and Gentlemen," chanted the announcer, "tonight we have Mollie and Laurie performing their death-defying *Stegosaurus* stunts. Welcome our brave and beautiful trick riders in their sequined silver and lavender regalia. Let them hear your love and excitement."

Big-footed clowns in baggy pants hopped around the arena, ready for a few laughs and to offer help in case of an emergency.

"Look at this pair of matching Steggies," declared the rodeo man with the microphone. They are taller than the cab of a cowboy's truck and each one weighs more than three steers. Some of them grow up to 30 feet long--longer than three pickup trucks parked end to end. Each fierce animal sports a set of dualie plates running right down the middle of his back. And look at those pointy spikes at the end of his great swishing tail!"

The crowd gasped. "You clowns be careful out there," cautioned the announcer. "If a Steggie swings his tail and catches you with a spike, he'll put out your lights." The crowd joined in a nervous "ooooh~~."

Two beautiful ladies in spangles and sparkles, each standing atop a fierce *Stegosaurus*, burst into the arena and glittered under the lights. With nothing more than decorative hoods on the beasts' little heads and ropes for the agile girls to grasp, the athletic trick riders controlled their cantankerous mounts.

They waved at the crowd the first time around. On their second trip around the arena, they turned, danced, and twirled between the animals' bony, back plates. One slip of a foot and their act would be finished. All the people in the stands held their breath and silently watched the risky performance.

As the Steggies galumphed around the arena in unison, they whipped their tails, they snarled, they snapped at each other. The graceful girls, performing dangerous tricks, thrilled the crowd.

"Oh, Jake, aren't they brave and beautiful? I want to be a Steggie stunt rider when I grow up."

"That's pretty chancy, Little Sister," counseled her big brother.

"Why don't you and your *Struthiomimus* practice hard on your barrel racing, instead? Remember, you and Strutty are in the finals tonight. If you run the barrels in fewer than 17 seconds without knocking one over, you will be the state barrel racing champ."

Levi knew she and Strutty could run those barrels in 17 seconds. "I'm strong, smart, and savvy," she declared, "and brave enough to spur Strutty to breakneck speed."

The trick riders made a grand finale ride. The Steggies clumped out of the big, swinging gates, back to their corrals behind the chutes.

"...and now--ladies and gentlemen, kids and dogs--it's time to prepare for the *Tyrannosaurus rex* saddle bronc event," blared the announcer, "the meanest--toughest--roughest event of the night."

Jake turned to his sister, "I've got to go now, Levi. It will take me a while to get ready to ride. This is my chance to be a champion dinosaur saddle bronc rider. Wish me luck."

The clowns rolled out their safety barrels and also cleaned up some dino droppings. The tractor man groomed the arena, and the friendly announcer entertained the crowd with a piece of local history.

"Long before our settlers claimed these sagebrush lands and before our cowboys and cowgirls were competing in this arena, the Indians roamed this desert. They called their village Toponis, which means Black Cherry. Today, the growth along the river is called chokecherry bushes, but we still use the original name of the village in logos, titles, and places around your town."

The band played the Toponis High fight song, a rousing tune signaling the arena was ready for the *T. rex* event. All those gigantic king lizards, banging and clanging in the chutes, reared up to their full 15 feet. They kept biting at one another over the metal gates, and bellowed loud and long. They made quite a ruckus!

The cowboys had their hands full putting saddle riggings and flank straps on each 40-foot dinosaur. It was not an easy job haltering a four-foot-long skull, hooking a rope under the dinosaur's chunky jaw bone, and running it up for the rider to grasp with one strong grip. Luckily, the dinosaur's short neck prevented the angry beast from biting the rider clinging to the back of the mighty *T. rex*.

"Watch out for those eight-inch teeth; all 58 of them are sharper than a drawer full of your mother's steak knives!" continued the announcer. "You're working on the Tyrant King, the orneriest of this bunch."

"Yeah, I'm, watching," answered the clown, and added, "that lizard's stinkin' breath makes me feel gaggy so I'm not cuddling up to him."

Jake climbed over the rails with his saddle slung over his shoulder. He threw it on the back of Tyrant King and tossed the cinch under the dinosaur's body, just in back of the great animal's little front legs.

"Hey, Rob," called Jake to his friend, "can you catch this cinch when I fling it?" It took two or three men to saddle a *T. rex*. Rob caught one end of the cinch and hooked it up tight on his side of the great beast.

"Ready, Jake!"

"Thanks, Pal." The young rider let himself down easy onto the saddle that was strapped to the red, dusty hide of the beast. Sky-high above the ground, straddling a giant dinosaur at a nearly straight-up angle took Jake's breath away.

With his gloved hand he pulled the halter rope tight and scooted his body around in the saddle until it felt just right. His chaps protected him from the dinosaur's rough hide.

"Let 'er rip!" he hollered, nodding his head.

Like a tight coil, Tyrant King sprang out of the chute. Jake spurred. The beast wrenched its body to the right, to the left. It teetered up and down, trying to shake the young cowboy off its back. Jake's head snapped back and forth. His white shirt reflected the lavender glow of the evening sky.

Tyrannosaurus rex bellowed and twisted. Jake gritted his teeth. His body flew up and hit back down in the saddle with a thud. For eight long seconds, boy and beast battled in the arena. The rider concentrated so hard he didn't even hear the cheering crowd.

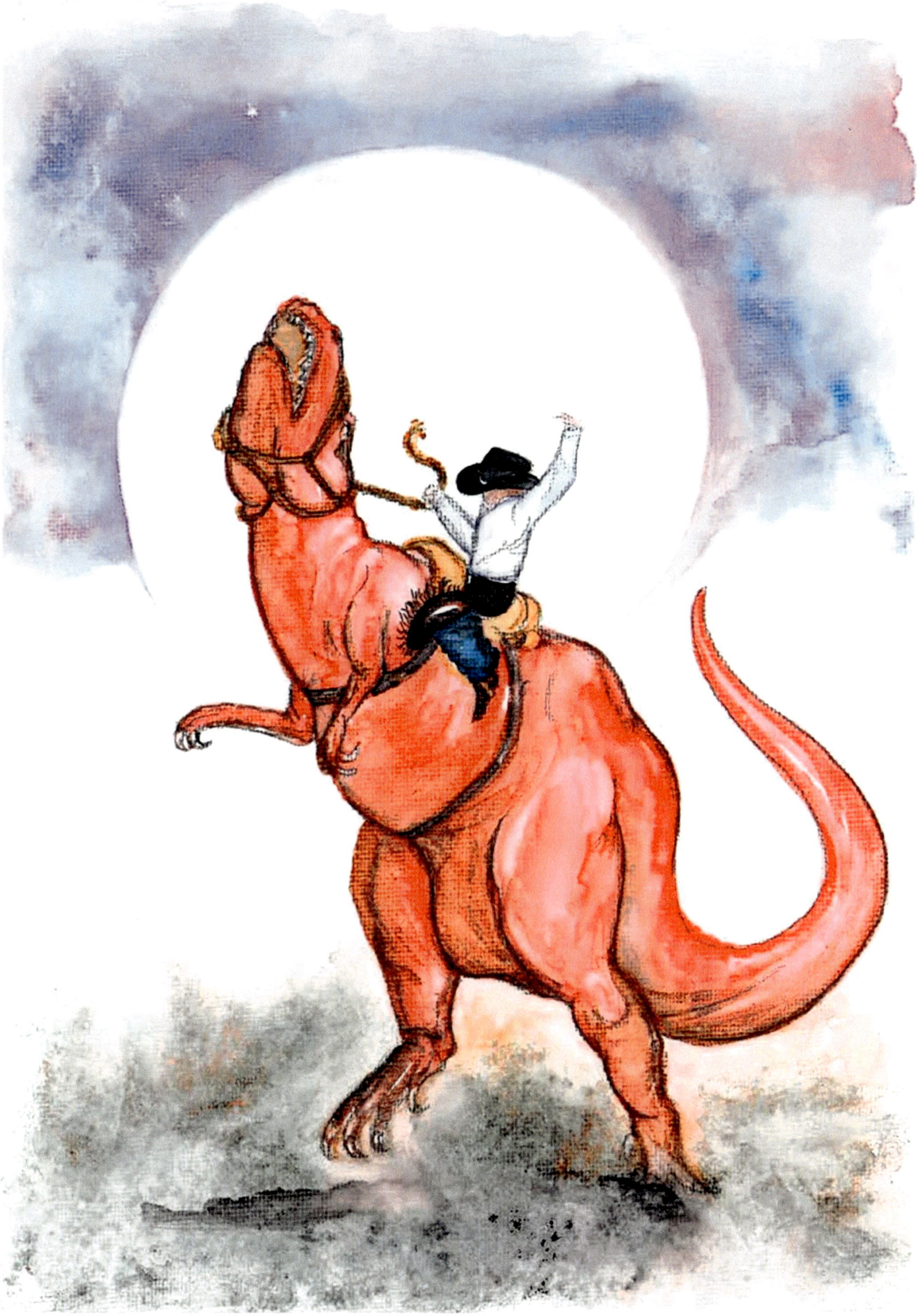

But he heard the buzzer squawk. Sliding backwards over the saddle, he let go of the rope, slid down the bulky back, and off the tip of the tail.

The spunky rider's feet hit the ground as angry Tyrant King lashed his massive tail and growled through the warm evening air. The roaring, guttural yawp rumbled across the sky, clear up to the Thunder Moon. Jake rolled out of danger's way just in the nick of time, but the swipe of the tail clipped the black felt cowboy hat off the boy's head.

The roaring crowd erupted to their feet--all together--like one giant explosion. They clapped--cheered--whistled--hooted --hollered--whooped. "Atta Boy," yelled the announcer.

The knuckles on Levi's clinched fists turned white. She couldn't believe how close Jake came to injury or maybe even death each time he rode.

The champ dusted off his shirt, picked up his hat, waved in victory to the cheering fans, and limped back to the chutes. It was then he discovered he had landed in a splat of dino droppings. Jake wondered if his footprints would be fossilized forever when the dino dung became a coprolite a million years later.

Jake and Levi perched on the fence and watched the rest of the *Tyrannosaurus rex* riders.

"Well, Little Levina," he started to say. . .

"**Don't** call me Levina!" demanded the feisty tomboy. "That is not the name I like."

"Sorry, sorry. I forgot. Guess that straight-up ride made all the blood drain out of my head. Anyway, Levi, you're up next, just as soon they finish this section of the *Tyrannosaurus* rides. There are only two riders left. Are you ready?"

"You Bet! I've been barrel racing on Strutty all summer, and we are ready to ride. Remember, we practiced two hours every day!" Butterflies and excitement tumbled in her stomach as she tightened her hat and swung into her saddle.

"Ladies and Gentlemen," crooned the announcer in his melodious voice, "gathered in this stadium tonight for your rodeo entertainment are some of the West's bravest, young lady barrel racers, each one competing on a mighty fine *Struthiomimus*. These girls are ready to ride for you." The microphone man declared, "Each one dares to ride like the wind, to spur her mount with confidence, and to sit in her saddle with power and purpose."

Changing his voice to an instructional tone, he explained, "*Struthiomimus* means Ostrich Imitator, and these dinosaurs do, indeed, run swift as ostriches. They are built lean, mean, and wiry, much like a lightweight horse. They run up to 35 miles per hour-- faster than the speed limit in your home town. Prepare yourselves for some record breaking times from these young lasses as they circle the barrels."

All the girls behind the chutes were talking to their mounts and patting their long necks.

"Our first racer tonight is Levi Lundlie riding her tawny-orange *Struthiomimus*, Strutty. They have practiced diligently all summer and right now she is in the running to win a gold buckle and the state barrel-racing title in her category. This all-around young lady is cheery as a summer's morning and determined as an Idaho wind storm. Let's bring her out with a hearty welcome from all you fine folks right here in Toponis County, Idaho!"

Levi and Strutty burst through the gate, revved-up and ready to run. Strutty pranced around the far end of the arena, jockeying for the right position. Her little front legs flopped around while her strong, gangly back legs pounded the ground, faster and faster.

Levi leaned forward in the saddle, spurred her mount and said, "Let's go girl!"

Arena dust flew up in fat puffs behind the speeding dinosaur. They cut the first barrel so close that it tipped, but didn't go over. They slid around the second barrel like a halo around the moon.

Beast and girl leaned into the third barrel. Levi spurred Strutty as they zipped around it clean and clear. The pair streaked down the straight-away, thundering into home.

"Ladies and Gentlemen," cheered the man behind the mike. "Your perky little barrel racer came home with a time of 16:48 seconds. With a time like that, this little lady won the night."

"Great ride, little sister!" hollered Jake as he hugged her. The bright Thunder Moon hung in the sky, shiny as Levi's new, gold trophy buckle.

Back behind the chutes, a corral full of fighting *Pentaceratops* milled around, bunting each other, winding up for the five-lap *Pentaceratop* races. A total of five long, sharp, curvy bones on the nose, over the eyes, and on the head of this magnificent dinosaur signaled warnings to approaching enemies. The beasts' splendid neck frills made of bone framed their ferocious faces and shielded them from attackers and enemies. The teams were saddling up for the exciting race, each one knowing he and his hefty dinosaur would win.

In another corral, armored *Ankylosaurus* lumbered slowly around in their pens, rooting the ground for food, awaiting the Heavyweight Pulling Contest. Large as tanks, the Fused Lizards wore bumpy, bony, body coverings. Armor even covered their eyelids.

Their long tails sported hard, bony clubs at the end with which they whomped and whacked their enemies. The drivers were wary as they prepared for the pulling contest. Drivers harnessed and hooked the cantankerous beasts to flat skids, each loaded with 11 ton of lava rocks. The first lumpish reptile to drag his load across the finish line at the other end of the arena won the title "Strongest Dino of All."

While the leery drivers checked their lava loads and harnesses one last time, the colorful clown hopped around like an Idaho jack rabbit, teasing the armored, lumpy dinos as the crowd egged him on.

"Hey, Mr. Funny Man," hollered the announcer, "this curious crowd sitting in the grandstand tonight wonders why you rodeo clowns always wear such LOUD stockings."

"Whoo-hoo. I'm glad you asked," replied the funny man pointing at his crazy colored socks. "We wear loud stockings so our feet don't fall asleep, "he answered, and giggled, "Tee-Hee. . . "

Over in the pens, far away from the chutes, three *Styracosaurus* banged on the steel panels. The ferocious animals, as antsy and restless as grouchy Brahma bulls, hooked their horns in the gates. The rattling and clanging of heavy steel panels echoed throughout the arena and up into the stands.

Every rodeo saved the *Styracosaurus* for the last act, right after the crowning of the new queen. Tonight, for the grand finale, all three spiked lizards would be turned loose so the clowns could taunt and tease them, much to the thrill of the audience.

Every time a spiked dinosaur chased a clown or missed the funny man by only a second, the audience gasped and cheered. If ever the horn of the vicious beast connected with a body, it meant curtains for the clown. Dangers and close calls always roused the stadium crowd into standing up and roaring, reminiscent of the Colosseum of old Rome.

"Ladies and Gentlemen, get ready now for our roping event," urged the microphone man. "We have five of the state's top ropers right here for your entertainment, and we are matching them with five of the best *Leptoceratop* dinosaurs on the circuit." The announcer reminded the crowd that these smaller dinos may look insignificant, . . ."but don't let their little size fool you. These horn-faced runners weigh up to half a ton and our cowboys have their work cut out for them."

Roping, a favorite event with the crowd, reminded the spectators of the early West when cowboys had to rope the dogies in order to brand them. Jake's *Allosaurus*, his well trained roping dinosaur-steed, trampled and stomped in the chute, ready to bolt out the gate without breaking the time barrier. Known as the King of Jurassic predators and called the Strange Reptile, the massive carnivore sported bony, three-clawed hands that looked big enough to clutch Jake's head with a vice-like grip. The daring young rider eased himself into his roping saddle as he talked to his mount, patted his neck, and calmed the beast's eagerness to run.

The Strange Reptile with powerful jaws and 70 sharp, thick teeth reminded all the cowboys of the dangers of dinosaur rodeoing. Every time a new dinosaur-wrangler came out swinging his lasso, energetic spectators hooted and hollered, spurring the roper on to a faster winning time.

"Our last *Leptoceratop* roper tonight is Jake Lundlie. If he makes the best time in this event, Ladies and Gentlemen, he will earn the title of all-around dinosaur wrangler." Drumming up excitement, the announcer spurred on the crowd, "Let's hear it for Jake . . ."

"Wish me luck, Levi," shouted the young roper from atop his saddled dinosaur-steed. "This is my big chance. Watch me rope that hooded Lepto."

Seconds later Jake dropped his lasso over the head of the bellowing *Leptoceratop.* "He did it, Ladies and Gentlemen!" cheered the announcer.

"Our champion roper and all-around dinosaur wrangler is Jacob Lundlie with a time of 5:9 seconds."

The band gave a drum roll; the summer evening settled in warm and breezy as the pick-up men herded the last roping dinosaur back to the holding pens.

"As soon as the arena is cleared," continued the voice on the mike, "we have some beautiful queen contestants eager to display their splendor and glory. . . . As we wait for our queens to make the last check of their regalia, the clown says he has one more important dinosaur to tell you about.

"Mr. Clown, please share your information with your eager listeners," said the announcer.

"Okay, Moms and Dads . . .Boys and Girls. . . ," declared the clown.

"What do you call a dinosaur with a big, huge, giant, mighty vocabulary? I'll give you ten seconds to answer my question."

The crowd chittered and chattered among themselves for a moment.

"Time's up, Folks," chortled the clown. "A dinosaur with a big vocabulary is called "A The-Saur-Us."

The crowd groaned and laughed when they realized the funny man was pulling their legs.

"Enough of your funny stuff, you capricious clown," chided the announcer. "Let's welcome our lovely queen contestants into the arena . . . Here they come now . . ."

First came three bantam *Pterodactyluses* flying in a row. These eagle-sized reptiles, trained as color guards, flew around the arena trailing brightly-colored streamers. Each one carried several fluttering ribbons clenched in its long, toothy bill. As they flew, dipped, and rose, the streamers wig-wagged far out behind them. A favorite cowboy song, "Back in the Saddle Again," played by the lively Toponis High Band blared over loudspeakers.

The winged *Pterodactyluses* finished their flight, ascended into the sky, and glided in circles above the crowd. Their streamers snapped in the warm, sage-scented evening breeze.

Immediately behind the color guard, five eager lasses flew in on *Pteranodons*. The contestants rode their well trained mounts and guided them with only a simple strap around the necks of the animals.

Levi, the last to ride the ring, had changed into her queening outfit. She wore pearly-black boots, pants and hat, accented with a shimmery pink shirt. Levi's outfit complimented the iridescent body of Anna, whose wings glistened in the moonlight.

Her 20-foot wings, as long as a cowboy's lasso, glimmered in the bright floodlights of the arena, reflecting the changing colors of the sunset.

As the girls swooped and glided on their graceful mounts, the clown shared a joke with the microphone man who repeated it to the crowd:

"Why will you never hear one of these P*teranadons* go to the bathroom?" asked the clown.

"We don't know," answered the announcer. "You tell us."

"Because the *"P"* is silent."

Again, some of the listeners chuckled; some groaned at the pun. All the little kids giggled and tittered at the clown's sort-of-naughty humor.

After the girls made their entry flight together, each one flew a ride by herself, showing off her mount and her Pteranodonmanship.

Levi hunkered down low between Anna's wings, neck-reined her flying reptile, and circled the ring at a 45-degree angle. Daringly, she flew so low that Anna's long, slender wingtip scooped a mark in the soft earth. Levi knew this risky pattern would earn extra points. The crowd felt the breezes stir as the spirited queen contestant whisked by.

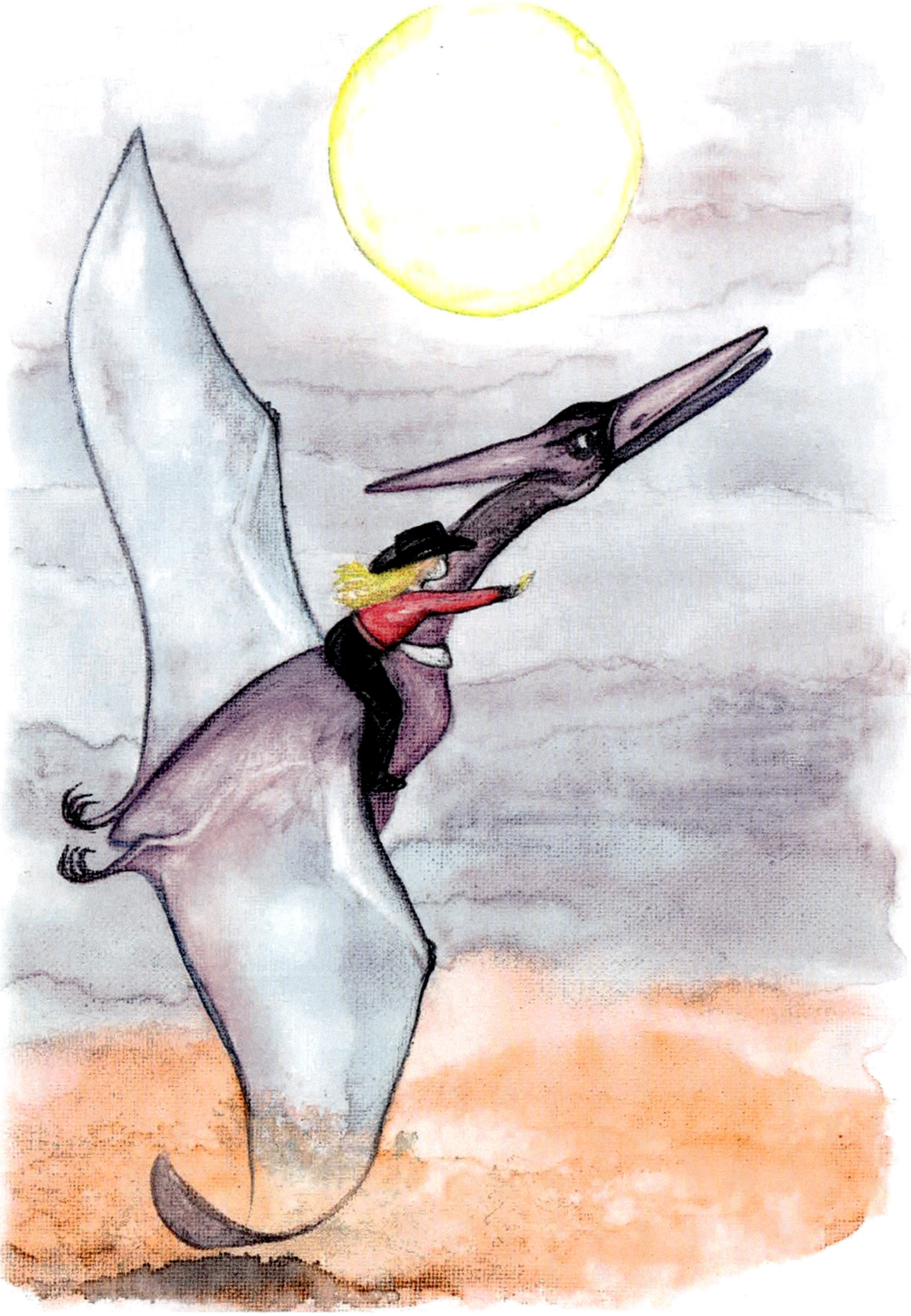

For Levi's presentation ride, her winged lizard tipped at a precarious angle toward the bleachers, giving them a full view of the rider. With a snappy flick of her wrist, Levi saluted her crowd off the brim of her hat.

When all the contestants finished their rides, they soared back into the arena together, circled the field, and settled into the dirt in perfect formation. The well-trained *Pteranadons* folded their wings into their sides and patiently perched in the sand.

Jake cheered when he heard the announcer declare, "Presenting our queen--Miss Levi Lundlie who comes from the town of Hailey, in your Great State of Idaho." Brother ran across the ring toward little sister. Levi slipped off Anna to receive her bouquet of roses and give Jake a hug. The high school band struck up an exuberant tune of triumph.

Out in the *Styracosaurus* holding pens, one of the wranglers heard cheering and music. He thought the queen contest had ended and the arena was clear, which was his signal to send out the gnarly beasts for the last act. Opening the gates, he herded the snorting lizards out of the corrals and down the alleyway.

Lean, mean, and always angry, the one-horned, spike-collared dinosaurs rumbled and bellowed toward the final gate. Cumbersome as combines, but faster than Quarter Horses, their dino power trembled the earth. Shoving, ramming, and butting, the monsters destroyed the sturdy wooden gate and exploded into the arena.

Screams erupted in the stands. The other four girls, still mounted, spurred their *Pteranodons* and rose into the air. Running as fast as they could, the vigilant clowns bolted in to distract the rambunctious, snarling beasts and protect Levi and Jake as they scrambled out of harm's way.

The nearsighted brutes beelined toward the sparkling, pink blur directly in their line of vision.

"Fly away, Levi! Jump on and fly away!" yelled Jake

"Come with me! Help me on!" screamed Levi.

Jake made a flying leap into the middle of Anna's back. Levi dropped her flowers, scattering petals behind her, and tried to scramble onto Anna.   Jake reached out for his little sister and their fingers touched. The lead *Styracosaurus* grazed Levi on the back side with the tip of his two-foot, killer horn causing a stingy, burning feeling along her leg.

With all his might, Jake leaned down and grabbed Levi's belt. Levi used his boot as a stirrup as he dragged her up on Anna's back.

The instant that faithful Anna felt the young girl's body settle on, the giant reptile flapped her strong wings and rose magnificently into the night sky, out of danger, and straight up toward the Thunder Moon.

Far below, they heard the cheering crowd. The sound faded away into the night. . . .

"I hear Mom and Dad coming," whispered Jake. "Let's not tell them what we did tonight. It would only make them worry."

In chorus, both kids hollered, "How did you do, Dad?"

"I won! Wish you had been there to help me out with a few of your good cheers. How was your evening? What did you do?"

"Oh, not much," mumbled Jake. "Everything was pretty quiet."

"Yeah, we just read a dinosaur book," added Levi, as she rubbed the tender spot on her back side. She could still feel her skin lightly tingle and burn.

Levi and Jake stole a glance outside. A shared secret flicked from eye to eye as Jake scraped a bit of dino dung off his boot and brushed some soft, brown dirt off his pant leg.

With the toe of her boot, Levi scuffed a single rose petal under the couch, out of sight.

They watched the entire herd of rodeo dinosaurs stampeding toward the Thunder Moon.

Pronunciation Guide

Allosaurus	al-oh-SORE-us	Strange Reptile
Ankylosaurus	AN-kye-loh-SORE-us	Fused Lizard
A Thesaurus	ah-the-SORE-us	A book of synonyms
Brontosaurus	bron-toe-SORE-us	Thunder Lizard
Coprolite	COP-rə-lite	Fossilized dino poop
Leptoceratops	LEP-toe-SERR-ah-tops	Slim Horned Face
Pentaceratops	PEN-ta-SER-ah-tops	Five-horned Face
Pteranodon	tə-RAN-ah-don	Winged and Toothless
Pterodactylus	TER-ah-DAK-təl-us	Winged Finger
Stegosaurus	STEG-oh-SORE-us	Roof Lizard
Struthiomimus	strooth-ee-oh-MY-mus	Ostrich Mimic
Styracosaurus	sty-RACK-oh-SORE-us	Spike Lizard
Tyrannosaurus rex	tye-RAN-oh-SORE-us	Tyrant Lizard King

Made in the USA
San Bernardino, CA
07 April 2018